★—————★ I'm ★—————★
George Washington,
and You're Not!

★—————————★—————————★—————————★

STEVEN KROLL

ILLUSTRATED BY
BETSY LEWIN

HYPERION BOOKS FOR CHILDREN

NEW YORK

For information address
Hyperion Books for Children,
114 Fifth Avenue, New York, New York 10011.
FIRST EDITION
1 3 5 7 9 10 8 6 4 2

Library of Congress Cataloging-in-Publication Data

Kroll, Steven
I'm George Washington, and you're not!/Steven Kroll;
illustrated by Betsy Lewin — 1st ed.
p. cm
Summary: Eric doesn't want to play George Washington
in the school play because he has stage fright,
but when Marty the class bully gets the part instead,
there's trouble ahead.
ISBN 1-56282-579-8 (trade) — ISBN 1-56282-580-1 (lib. bdg.)
[1. Stage fright — Fiction. 2. Acting — Fiction. 3. Self-
confidence — Fiction. 4. Schools — Fiction. 5. Washington's
Birthday — Fiction.] I. Lewin, Betsy, ill. II. Title.
PZ7.K9225Im   1994
[Fic] — dc20   93-7536   CIP   AC

For Norma Fox and Harry Mazer
—S.K.

Contents

1. A Play for George Washington . . . 1
2. Another Tree . . . 8
3. Moans and Shrieks . . . 16
4. Sour Grapes? . . . 24
5. Good as Gold? . . . 32
6. The Cafetorium Is Full of People! . . . 40
7. Curtains . . . 49

★ 1 ★
A Play for George Washington

Eric walked into class. Mrs. Connors, his teacher, was up in front of the room. She was about to make an important announcement.

Everyone got very quiet. Quickly Eric slid into his seat. Across the room, his friend Danny Fontina grinned hello.

Mrs. Connors cleared her throat and smoothed her hair. "Class," she asked, "whose birthday is coming up on February 22nd?"

Sitting in the front row, Rosy Martinez

1

began waving her hand. "George Washington's, Mrs. Connors!"

"And do we all know who George Washington was?"

Henry Woo raised his hand. "The first president of the United States."

"Very good, Rosy. Very good, Henry. Now I have a surprise for all of you. To celebrate George Washington's birthday, I have written a play about his life that we're going to perform. I've made a list of what everyone will do."

Eric's throat went dry. His heart pounded. Oh, please, not a speaking part, he thought. I do all right with the other kids in class, but I hate getting up in front of an audience.

Mrs. Connors began writing on the blackboard.

Costumes: Judy Hanson
British officer: Henry Woo

American officer: Miranda Jackson
Chief tree: Danny Fontina
George Washington: Eric Mills

Henry and Miranda gasped, but Eric felt sick to his stomach. He broke out in a sweat. When Mrs. Connors finished writing, the other kids with parts went up to get their scripts. Eric just sat at his desk.

Danny tugged at his sleeve. "Hey, Eric, you're George Washington. You have to get your script."

"Oh . . . sure," Eric said.

He stumbled forward. As he accepted his script from Mrs. Connors, she smiled. "Congratulations, Eric. I think you'll be a wonderful George Washington."

Eric looked at the floor. "Thanks, Mrs. Connors."

He wanted to disappear into his desk, disappear into the ground. He didn't want

to be George Washington. He didn't want to be in a play at all!

The day went by in a blur. Arithmetic was a sea of numbers, language arts a jumble of words. At recess, he was usually the captain of a team. Today, he hung around while the other kids played kickball. In music, he helped pass out the songbooks but forgot to sing along with "Home on the Range."

Finally, it was time to go. Eric scooped up the books he knew he'd need that night and put them in his backpack. He got into line with the other kids and ran for the school bus the moment Mrs. Connors said, "Dismissed."

He sat in the back, trying to avoid everyone, but Danny found him anyway. Over the bus seats, he could see Danny's dark hair—so much darker than his own—bobbing all the way down the aisle.

Danny sat next to him. "So what's going

on with you? You've been really weird all day."

Eric looked straight ahead. "I don't want to be George Washington."

"Why not? You'll be great."

"I don't like acting. I don't want to be on a stage."

"But it's neat, and you're the best one for the part. You even look a little like George Washington."

"I do not. George Washington was old, and he wore a wig."

Danny laughed. "That's not what I meant. Your nose, your face . . ."

"I don't care. I won't do it."

"I know you *can*, but if you don't want to, you could always be a tree. Mrs. Connors would let you."

Eric looked over at Danny. "A tree, like you!"

"Yes. We could do lots of leafy things together."

Eric smiled. A tree would have no lines
to forget and a tree costume to hide
behind.

He clapped his hands and shot a fist in
the air. "I could be a tree!"

★ 2 ★
Another Tree

When the school bus dropped Eric off in front of his house, he ran up the steps, pushed open the door, and headed for his room.

Halfway there, he heard his mother say, "Is that you, Eric?"

"Yes, Mom. Is it okay if I stay by myself for a while?"

"Sure. Dinner's at seven. Are you all right?"

"Yeah. I just need to think about some things."

He closed the door, took off his backpack, and threw himself on the bed. For a long time he stared at the ceiling.

He and Danny had joked some more about being trees, but would Mrs. Connors let him out of being George Washington? Besides, wouldn't it be embarrassing to give up the leading role for a part with no lines?

Eric thought about this. Maybe he shouldn't be a tree. He could make scenery or be in charge of props, anything that wouldn't mean going onstage.

That was what he couldn't tell Danny. It wasn't only that he didn't like acting or didn't want the part. Stepping into that big open space with all those people looking on—he got scared just imagining being out there.

But being a tree with Danny might be fun. . . .

"Eric!"

"Coming, Mom."

He washed his hands, said hi to his parents, and sat down at the dining room table. Dinner was meat loaf, noodles, and peas with mushrooms. He liked everything, but it was hard to concentrate. He picked at the meat loaf and pushed a few peas around his plate.

His parents ate their food, watched him, and looked at each other. All you could hear were the knives and forks making cutting and scooping noises on their plates. Finally Mom said, "Please tell us what's the matter."

Eric swallowed hard. He couldn't look up. "Mrs. Connors wrote a play about George Washington. She wants me to be him."

"The lead in the class play!" Dad said. "That's terrific, Eric!"

"We know Mrs. Connors thinks a lot of you," said Mom.

Eric's eyes blurred. "I don't like acting!" he yelled. Then he got up from the table and ran to his room.

Mom and Dad followed. When he had stopped crying, Eric admitted he was scared to go onstage.

"Lots of actors have stage fright," Dad replied. "You have to work at it, make it go away."

"I can't," Eric said. "I just don't want to be out there."

"Sweetie," said Mom, "we understand how you feel, but if someone tried to help you, do you think—"

"No!"

"In that case," Dad said, "you'd better tell Mrs. Connors tomorrow."

"Okay," Eric said, and immediately felt better. He even went back and ate some of his dinner. By the time he'd finished his homework and was ready for bed, he knew he'd get a good night's sleep.

Before school began the next morning, Eric took a deep breath, marched to the front of the room, and said, "I don't want to be George Washington, Mrs. Connors."

She looked upset. "But you're such a good leader, Eric, and you have such a nice voice. George Washington has to sing 'Yankee Doodle.' That's one of the reasons I picked you for the part."

Eric blushed. "I can't sing in front of people. I get too scared." Then, suddenly, in a rush, "Maybe I could be a tree, like Danny!"

"Well, all right. You can be a tree, and I'll assign the part of George Washington to Marty Boomer. He's the only other possible choice, I'm afraid, but I *am* sorry. I know you would have done a wonderful job."

Eric's face fell. Oh no, he thought. Not Marty Boomer, the class show-off! But at least he was off the hook, and who could

tell? Maybe Marty Boomer would be good. Now he had to concentrate on trying to be a tree. He'd still have to be onstage. . . .

"Thanks, Mrs. Connors," Eric said. Then he ran off to tell Danny the good news.

★ 3 ★

Moans and Shrieks

That afternoon, everyone began preparing for the play. Richard Kim, head of scenery, took his group off to the art room in search of poster board and paint. At the back of the classroom, Judy Hanson led her group in making sketches of what the costumes would look like. Up front, the kids with speaking parts rehearsed on one side of the room, and the trees rehearsed on the other.

There were three trees: Danny, Eric, and Rosy Martinez. Mrs. Connors explained that they would each have a cardboard cutout to stand behind. Each cutout would have a handle to hold so it would be easy to keep upright and move around. The trees would be in different positions on the stage in different scenes. Most of the time they would be quiet and motionless, but with the soldiers at Valley Forge, they would have to rock from side to side and moan about how cold it was.

Mrs. Connors demonstrated the rocking and moaning, swaying back and forth with her hands clasped in front of her and her eyes closed. The clasped hands were supposed to represent the tree she was holding.

The three trees found it hard not to laugh. But then Mrs. Connors finished and was smoothing her long brown hair.

"You three practice what I've shown you," she said. "I'm going over to work with the actors who have speaking parts."

Eric felt a little pang. Then the three trees looked at one another and giggled.

"Who's going to go first?" Danny asked.

"Not me," said Rosy.

"Not me," said Eric.

"Well, it's certainly not going to be *me*!" Danny said.

"I know," said Eric, "why don't we all try together?"

"A genius," said Danny. "What a good idea."

The three trees lined up. They clasped their hands in front of them and rocked from side to side.

"Brr, it's cold!" moaned Rosy.

"Oooh, I'm freezing!" moaned Eric.

"Brr, brr, I've got goose bumps!" moaned Danny.

"You mean you've got bark bumps," Eric whispered.

"Brr, brr, I've got bark bumps!" moaned Danny.

Within minutes, they were bumping into each other and laughing hysterically. Mrs. Connors hurried over.

"Children," she said, hands on hips, "can't I leave you alone for a moment? You were supposed to be practicing. . . ."

"We *were* practicing, Mrs. Connors," said Danny. "It's just—"

"Maybe it will be easier when we have the trees," said Eric, a little breathless from so much laughing.

"All right now, you three," said Mrs. Connors, "please settle down. Danny, you're chief tree. Make sure everyone does it right. I have to help the others!"

Danny watched her walk away. He folded his arms. "All right, let's do it."

The three trees got back in line. Soon they were rocking and moaning, rocking and moaning. It didn't take long to get the knack.

They finished practicing, sat down, and began watching the rehearsal across the room.

It was the scene between George and

Martha Washington at Mount Vernon. Little Beth Polsky surprised everyone with her big speaking voice. She made a great Martha.

"Please stand beside Beth, Marty," said Mrs. Connors.

But Marty Boomer wouldn't. He skipped around her, shrieking and pumping his fist. "IIIIIII'm George Washington!" he shouted.

"Marty, stop it!" said Mrs. Connors, but Marty wouldn't stop. Then he stood beside Beth and tried to tickle her.

"Marty!" cried Mrs. Connors. "In another moment I will send you to the principal's office!"

Marty stood still, but the scene didn't go very well. When they began to rehearse Valley Forge, he was off again, shouting, stamping, upstaging everyone, and romping around on a bright yellow hobbyhorse. Nothing Mrs. Connors said or did could

make any difference, and when it was time for him to sing "Yankee Doodle," he snorted and sang off-key on purpose.

With rehearsal over and school letting out, Eric and Danny went to get their parkas. As Eric reached for his, he felt someone bump his shoulder. He turned, and there was Marty Boomer.

Marty smirked and put his thumbs in his armpits. "Look who's George Washington now!" he gloated, and stuck out his tongue.

★ 4 ★
Sour Grapes?

At dinner that night, Eric was still bewildered. As he bent over his chicken cutlet, his mom asked how everything had gone.

Eric looked up. "Oh, fine. I'm a tree now."

"A tree?" said Dad.

"Yes," said Eric. Then he explained about Mrs. Connors and Danny and the rehearsal of the three trees. He was going to stop there, but he couldn't. He told the whole story of Marty Boomer and how awful he was.

"Oh, Eric," said his mom. She came over and hugged him.

That made him feel a little better. Then Dad said, "Do you think you should have kept the part?"

Eric blinked and swallowed hard. He'd been wondering the same thing all afternoon. Would the play be a flop now that Marty Boomer was George Washington? Would it be *his* fault if that happened? Would Marty, knowing he was second choice, never leave Eric alone?

"No," Eric said. "I couldn't have played George Washington. Not even Marty Boomer could make me want to play him."

"Well, at least you're sure," Dad said. "Could anything change your mind?"

Eric shook his head. "I'm even nervous about being a tree."

Before lunch the following afternoon, Mrs. Connors made another announcement. "At rehearsal today, class, the three trees will rehearse with those who have speaking parts. The trees must learn their

places in different scenes, and after George Washington has sung the first verse of 'Yankee Doodle,' everyone onstage will sing the chorus."

Oh boy, thought Eric. Over lunch he asked Danny what he thought rehearsing with Marty would be like.

Danny choked on his milk. He rolled his eyes and coughed.

Things got off to a pretty good start, though, mostly because Marty wasn't even in the first scene. It involved George Washington's boyhood home and interests, and the kids onstage read carefully from the script and listened to what Mrs. Connors said to do. Eric and Danny were right up front, and Rosy was back near the painting of the house. As the scene ended, Eric noticed Marty squirming around in his seat.

Mrs. Connors asked everyone to get ready for the next scene, the French and Indian War. Before Debby Rabinowitz

could read her narrator's introduction, Marty jumped on his yellow hobbyhorse, waved his wooden sword in the air, and chased the group of terrified French soldiers all over the classroom.

"Marty, stop it!" shouted Mrs. Connors.

Marty paid no attention. "Charge!" he yelled, and galloped down the aisle.

Mrs. Connors grabbed him by the collar. "Enough is enough! If you continue to carry on like this, there will be no play."

Marty's shoulders slumped. He looked almost sheepish. "Okay, Mrs. Connors."

Then he straightened up and walked back to the rehearsal area, smiling happily.

The French and Indian War went fine. Unbelievably, so did George and Martha at home at Mount Vernon. But by the time Valley Forge rolled around, Marty Boomer was once again finding it hard to behave himself.

When Miranda Jackson, playing the

American officer, asked about lifting the spirits of the soldiers, Marty tried to poke her. When Henry Woo, playing the British officer, went to capture George Washington, Marty refused to stay captured. He fought and kicked and ran right into Rosy Martinez.

Mrs. Connors made sure Henry and Rosy were all right. Then she waggled her index finger at Marty. "Marty, this is your last chance. One more outburst, and I am not only stopping the play, I am calling your mother and sending you home!"

Marty smiled grimly, almost as if he were pleased to be so important that all those things could be done to him. "Yes, Mrs. Connors" was all he said.

The rest of the scene at Valley Forge went practically like clockwork. At the end, when Marty had to sing "Yankee Doodle," he did a really good job. Singing with the chorus, he went a little flat, but now, at least, he was making an effort.

Afterward, Eric, Danny, Henry, and Miranda gathered near the coat hooks. "Do you think Marty will be okay now?" Henry asked.

Danny shrugged. "I doubt it. He knows Mrs. Connors won't want to stop the play. He'll just wait till she's not looking. Then watch out!"

Miranda frowned. "Even when he's doing things right, I don't trust him. You just know he's got something awful on his mind."

"But maybe he'll listen," Eric said. "Those things Mrs. Connors said could make a difference."

"Oh yeah?"

It was Marty. He stepped in front of Eric and sneered. "Just so you know, I'm George Washington, and you're not!"

Then he stamped on Eric's f stormed away.

"Ow!" Eric said, and hopped ove chair.

"That creep!" said Danny.

"I told you what a louse he was," s Miranda.

But Eric was angry. Everyone kne Marty was George Washington only be cause Eric had refused the part. He wanted to rub Marty's nose in that, but, of course, he couldn't. It would sound too much like sour grapes.

★5★
Good as Gold?

At dinner he was glad that nothing came up about the play. The next afternoon, there was a rehearsal for speaking parts only, so he got to go to art and draw anything he wanted. Of course, he chose to draw trees. He hadn't seen his cardboard tree yet and was wondering what it would look like.

Danny made pictures of trees, too, tall spindly ones with just a few leaves on top. They were very different from Eric's big shaggy trees—trees big enough to hide in.

The following morning, Mrs. Connors

announced that George McGrath's poster committee had finished the posters. Before schoolwork began, George would divide the class into teams of two.

George stood. "Each team will have two posters to put up," he said.

Eric was paired with Miranda. Their posters were to go at the school entrance. One of them said Come to the Play and showed a big red stage with blue and yellow actors on it. The other said George Washington Lives! It had a picture of George Washington that looked a lot like pouty-faced Marty Boomer.

Eric held the first poster flat so Miranda could attach a loop of tape at each corner. Then they each grabbed an end and stuck the poster on the tile wall.

They were about to repeat the process with the second poster when Miranda dropped her end. "Oh, yuk," she said.

"That face, I can't stand it! Couldn't you be George Washington, Eric? You'd be so good!"

Eric was flattered. "Thanks, Miranda," he replied, "I wish I could have done it, but I couldn't. You'll see, Marty will be okay. He could give a really good performance."

Eric knew this was pushing it. Marty wouldn't be better than okay. But someone had to be George Washington, and there wasn't anyone else!

Miranda shook her head. "That kid, I'm telling you . . ."

They put up the other poster and walked back to class.

The days went swiftly by. Richard Kim's group got the scenery finished. Judy Hanson's group completed the costumes. There were rehearsals and more rehearsals. Miraculously, Marty Boomer had stopped misbehaving and even remembered his lines.

In what seemed like no time at all, Mrs. Connors announced that the next afternoon, Thursday, would be dress rehearsal. Unfortunately it would have to be in the classroom because the cafetorium was not available. She was not happy, but they would make do.

The cast got changed in the boys' and girls' bathrooms. Miranda looked sharp in her blue uniform with lots of buttons. Henry practically disappeared into his red one. Both of them looked a little weird in their wigs, and Marty ran around, pounding his onto his head. It was too small, but no one was going to tell him.

Eric was delighted with his cardboard tree, which was almost as shaggy as his drawing. He and Danny did a little jousting with trees before the performance began.

When it did begin, it was wonderful! In her white dress, Beth Polsky was charming as Martha Washington. Debby Rabinowitz made a great narrator, Henry and Miranda were letter-perfect, and everything Marty did, from chasing the French to singing "Yankee Doodle," came out fine.

Marty's going to do great, Eric thought as he and Danny and Rosy moved their trees from scene to scene. He got so excited, he forgot about his stage fright. Of course, they were still just in the classroom. . . .

Afterward, Mrs. Connors applauded them all. "You were as good as gold!" she said. "I can't wait to see you in the cafetorium tomorrow."

Eric saw Miranda frowning. He walked over.

"You don't think we were as good as gold?"

"We've still got tomorrow," Miranda said.

Eric nodded and turned toward the door. As he reached the hall, someone plowed into him.

"You were a lousy tree!" Marty Boomer hissed. Then he ran off to the boys' bathroom to change his costume.

Eric watched him go. They still had tomorrow, all right.

★6★
The Cafetorium
Is Full of People!

At breakfast Eric could hardly eat.

"Just try to relax," his mom said.

"Take a deep breath before you go on," said his dad.

"You'll be behind the cardboard tree the whole time," Mom said.

"You don't have to do much," said Dad.

None of this made any difference. Eric imagined being out on that huge stage in the cafetorium, where he had never been. He imagined the lights and all those people in the audience.

"We'll be there cheering for you," said Mom.

That was part of the trouble. If he did something wrong, his parents would see!

Somehow he managed to get himself on the school bus. Danny was there, looking a little nervous himself.

"You all ready?" he asked.

Eric shrugged.

Backstage, Mrs. Connors was handing out the costumes. Boys got changed in the wings on one side of the cafetorium. Girls got changed on the other.

Marty Boomer had come early. He was already in costume and bouncing around on his yellow hobbyhorse. He bounced in front of Henry and the other redcoats. He bounced in front of Eric and Danny, who were standing holding their trees. Then he bounced across the stage to bother the girls.

"Marty, get out of here!" yelled Mrs.

Connors, and he came bouncing back to the boys' side. If he was being a pest already, how would he behave onstage?

The cast gathered behind the curtain.

"You know," said Danny, "I'm really pretty nervous."

"Nervous!" said Eric. "I'm so scared, I can hardly stand up!"

Miranda peeked out at the audience. "The cafetorium is full of people!"

Eric thought his stomach would turn over and fall out on the floor, but just then the curtain rose. He and Danny and Rosy took their positions as a painting of George Washington's boyhood home was unrolled in the background.

When the three trees were in place, Debby Rabinowitz stepped forward.

"George Washington, the father of our country, was born on February 22, 1732. He grew up on a farm in Virginia."

Eric was way up front. As his classmates

42

described how young George Washington liked fishing and riding, arithmetic and surveying, he peered around the edge of his tree.

The audience was a sea of faces. Out there in the dark were his parents, but he couldn't find them. He wished he were somewhere else.

At least the first scene was now over. The backdrop painting changed to the French and Indian War. The trees moved closer to it, along with a row of French soldiers. Debby Rabinowitz stepped forward once again.

"Between 1754 and 1763, the English fought the French on American soil. George Washington commanded Virginia's army—"

At that moment George Washington came bouncing out of the wings. He crashed into Debby and knocked her down. "Charge!" he shouted, and galloped

across the stage. He chased away the French soldiers, ran his sword through the paper backdrop, and dashed off again.

The audience was stunned. Eric was furious. He could see Mrs. Connors lecturing Marty over to one side, but would that make any difference? A little shaken, Debby got up and completed her line.

"He helped the English win the war."

The scene changed to Mount Vernon.

The trees moved close to George and Martha, who were standing before their home. Cautiously, Debby walked to centerstage.

"On January 6, 1759, George Washington married Martha Custis, a young widow with two small children. For the next sixteen years, he remained a Virginia planter, enjoying his family and—"

"Ouch!" Beth Polsky shouted. "You stop that, Marty!"

She twisted away, stumbling in her white dress. Marty stood there in his uniform, laughing behind his hand.

The audience was laughing, too, but Eric had seen Marty pinch Beth Polsky. He was even angrier than before as Beth blushed and spoke her line.

"The harvest has been very good this year, George. You've done a wonderful job, looking after everything."

"Thank you, Martha," said George. "This weekend, let's have some friends in for dancing."

★7★
Curtains

Debby waved the actors offstage. A backdrop showing the tents and snow at Valley Forge took the place of Mount Vernon. American soldiers, looking cold and hungry, lay in front of it. George McGrath's pup tent appeared beside them. The three trees drifted forward.

Debby said, "The English began forcing the colonists to pay taxes they felt were unjust. In April 1775, fighting broke out at Lexington and Concord, Massachusetts. George Washington was chosen commander in chief of the American

Continental army. By the winter of 1777–78, the war was not going well."

The three trees rocked from side to side.

"Brr, it's cold!" moaned Rosy.

"Ooh, I'm freezing!" moaned Eric.

"Brr, brr, I've got bark bumps!" moaned Danny.

Eric gulped. He'd moaned onstage and lived! But what about Marty Boomer?

Eric looked around. So far so good. George Washington was standing in front of his soldiers, but nothing had gone wrong.

Miranda Jackson, American officer, approached him.

"We must find some way to lift the spirits of these men."

George Washington made a sweeping gesture and knocked off Miranda's wig. "Come to my tent and talk."

Miranda snatched up her wig and plopped it back on her head as Henry Woo,

British officer, jumped from behind a tree and grabbed George Washington.

"You are my prisoner!"

"No, I'm not!" said George Washington. He elbowed Henry in the ribs and fought his way free.

"Let General Washington go!" said Miranda, though clearly he was no longer caught.

"Get the enemy!" shouted the soldiers.

Three leaped up and grabbed the British officer. "Have mercy! I'll join the American army!" Henry wailed.

George Washington slapped Henry on the back so hard, he knocked him down.

"This officer has joined our side," George Washington declared. "He is a true patriot!"

"But we're patriots, too!" said the three heroic soldiers.

"Let's get ready to fight and win!" shouted the rest.

With that, George Washington began galloping around the stage. He waved, bowed, blew kisses, and was about to start singing "Yankee Doodle" when he tripped over Henry Woo's carefully placed out-stretched foot. In a moment he was flying through the air. In another moment he had landed in the laps of the parents in the front row!

The audience roared. The curtain came crashing down, but one lone tree was left in view. The tree was Eric.

Oh no! he thought.

Mrs. Connors began frantically playing the piano. "Sing, Eric, sing!"

Eric stepped from behind his tree. He picked up George Washington's hat, placed it on his head, and began.

> Yankee Doodle went to town,
> Riding on a pony,
> Stuck a feather in his cap
> And called it macaroni.
>
> Yankee Doodle, keep it up,
> Yankee Doodle dandy,
> Mind the music and the step,
> And with the girls be handy.

The music ended. Eric looked around. Incredibly, he was still alone onstage.

"It's up to you!" Mrs. Connors whispered.

Eric smiled. He'd been so angry at Marty, he was no longer afraid. He took a deep breath.

"George Washington became the first president of the United States in 1789. He served two terms and went home. Then he died."

The audience loved him. They cheered and clapped. Then the curtain went up, the rest of the cast crowded forward for their bows, and Mrs. Connors came rushing to the stage with a bouquet of flowers. She handed the flowers to Eric.

Puzzled, pleased, so relieved it was all over, Eric squinted into the lights. He was looking for his parents, but he still couldn't find them.

Mrs. Connors put her arm around his shoulder. "You saved the day. Next year you can play Abe Lincoln for Lincoln's birthday."

Eric found his parents and waved. He smiled up at Mrs. Connors. "Only if I can play him as a tree," he said.